M. Krueger

PORN STAR ALICE
AND
THE DILDO OF DOOM

1

Alice looked at them where they lay arrayed on a long, cloth-covered table like a row of surgical instruments. At one end lay a specimen so modest it might almost be called an embarrassment to its kind. Not to say she could pick her teeth with it, but it might have been bundled together with a few others of the same size without posing any real inconvenience.

At the other end of the table lay one that looked like it had better been shot out of a submarine or dropped from the belly of an airplane. At that moment, as she looked at it, there was no question in her mind that it had been cast purely for novelty purposes, as a thing to display on a pedestal like an objet d'art or to hang up as an antomatical facsimile on the wall of a science museum.

It was, for what it was worth, a lifelike specimen, right down to the molding of the veins and the overall complexion. But there was no question that it was impractical. And she had no idea why it had been set alongside those other, more workaday instruments.

In fact, the dildos arranged so neatly on the white tablecloth comprised a sort of scientific gradation from the unassuming fifty-caliber cartridge at one end to the howitzer shell at the other. If she hadn't known better, she would've thought it the booth for a dealer at a sex toy trade show. But it wasn't. It was the sound stage for My Goodness Productions on day one of shooting for her latest porno gig.

Alice had been doing pornos for a year now, as a side job. She had day work as a secretary for a law firm but was saving up money to study as a veterinarian. She was careful. She didn't take any jobs that didn't involve protection. It was no good becoming an animal doctor if she had to contract a disease to get it.

And so far, things had worked out as well as could be expected in an admittedly odd line of work. A business so disreputable brought in all sorts but she kept her distance, didn't socialize much, and always played the part of a professional.

The one person she couldn't quite keep her distance from was J. Gerald Peterson, commonly known as Jerry, the CEO of My Goodness, and the inevitable producer, writer and director of its films.

She was still wondering over the gargantuan dildo when Jerry caming striding across the room to meet her.

"I see you've met Big Bertha."

"Yes. Why is it here?"

"That should be obvious. You're going to use it."

"No, I'm not."

"Of course, you are. That's why you're here. Look, you should be glad. I know you. You're finicky. The further you can keep from bodily fluids, the better. Well, the only bodily fluid you're going to be in contact with for this show is your own. There are a few talking scenes with other actors—mostly you telling them that you're very busy, have a headache, and can't possible go out tonight. But for everything else, you'll be alone. With these." He gestured expansively at the armaments on the table.

"No. I won't. I mean, I can't. I mean, look at it. You've seen me naked before. Do you think I could possibly get that thing inside me?"

"Yes. Look, suppose I handed you a newborn baby and told you to stick it up your vagina. You'd think I was crazy, right?"

"Yes."

"And yet just a little while before, some woman was squeezing that baby *out* of her vagina. And Bertha isn't anywhere near as big as a newborn baby."

"Actually, it looks pretty close. And you're leaving out the part about how the woman giving birth was in agonizing pain."

"Right. I thought of that. Look, when a woman gives birth, she's not accustomed to having anything inside her but the usual sort of equipment. In fact, maybe even not that, since I doubt women are having a lot of sex in their third trimester. So it's probably less accommodating than it would be if they weren't pregnant at all."

"What's your point?"

"My point is that we're going to work you up gradually. You'll start down at that end—" He pointed in the direction of the .50-cal. "—and work your way to this end." He indicated the bunker buster.

"That's great. But seriously, it looks painful. I don't know if I want to do this. And I also don't know *why* you want me to do this. What's the point?"

"The point is, we're in an arms race. Time was, you could make a porno—maid's outfit, money shot, you're done. That's all it took. Now, though, there's porn everywhere. A little sex doesn't even mean anything anymore. And it's free. Anybody can see porn for nothing. Everything's devalued. And if you want people to pay for it, you've got to come with something special, new. That's why I've been ramping up the high concepts for our films. And look, if you really don't want to do this, we've got another starting up on the stage next door. I can probably swap you out with Christie."

"What's that one about?"

He explained it.

She put her face in her hands.

Jerry nodded. "That's what I figured. That's why I put you on this one. Listen to me, it's not going to be that bad. You'll work your way up a little at a time. We've got a month to shoot, a couple of hours a day. You'll have lubricant. And we're going to have a nurse on hand for the last few scenes."

"What's a nurse going to do?"

"Well, she can help if you get stuck. Besides, we've got this."

He walked over to a box and held up an instrument that she didn't recognize.

"What's that?"

"A jar lifter. They use them for canning. If it gets stuck— and I don't think it will—we just grab hold of it like this." He clamped the jar lifter on to the dildo and lifted it. He shook it over his head to show how firmly the lifter gripped it.

"That's how you'll get it out of me."

"If we have to, yeah. Between this, the lubricant, and a little twisting back and forth, it ought to slide out like a stick of butter."

Alice looked at him. He was grinning and holding the giant dildo beside his head with the jar lifter.

She crossed her arms. "The ones beside it aren't exactly small. What if I can't even work with them?"

"Not a problem. I've got an alternate ending written up for just that scenario. All through the movie, you're going to have these things stowed away in a cabinet. And every time you get one out, we're going to show the big ones, tease the audience with it, you know. So if you get stopped, we'll have a scene with you weeping because of the impossibilty of achieving your dream of diddling yourself with the big guns. And since you can't consummate your passion, you'll set up a shrine for them, place flowers around them and talk to them in hushed, worshipful tones like household gods. Trust me, I've got it all planned out. So don't worry. I don't expect you to do the impossible. Just do your best."

2

She got the script and read over the first scene. Unlike a lot of movies, most of the scenes were to be shot in order. This was partly because there were no special effects that needed to be tackled up front but also because of the exigencies of this film's peculiar project. They were, in Jerry's words, going for a world record.

It would literally be a world record. The largest dildos had been custom ordered and made according to specification. No woman had ever used dildos this big before.

As for the first scene, her boyfriend calls her on her cell phone. He wants to take her out to dinner. But she can't. She's not feeling well. He's disappointed to hear that. This is two nights in a row she's begged off. She's very sorry. But maybe tomorrow.

The real reason she put him off is that she was waiting for a package. And that afternoon, it arrives.

When the delivery man departs, she puts down a rather large box in the living room and tears it open. She digs through it, foam peanuts spilling out onto the floor, and draws from it a smaller box. From that box, she removes, one by one, a succession of dildos, placing each of them upright on the coffee table beside her.

The script emphasized that she was to remove them FROM SMALLEST TO LARGEST. When she got down to the last one, she was to pause and gasp, then hold it up in front of her face in an admiring way before kissing and caressing it. Then she was to place each of them in a wooden cabinet and give them one last gaze of pleasure before selecting the smallest of the bunch and retiring STAGE RIGHT.

That was it. No sex, no nudity. Virtually the whole scene was an unboxing. That made her think. She'd heard you could make real money posting unboxing videos online, showing people the latest and greatest toys and gadgets. Maybe she start a channel. It sounded easier than porn.

She got out of makeup and wardrobe, and waited to start. As she stood there, she thought of what she was in for. Could she do this? Did she want to do it? In theory, it should be harmless. Like Jerry said, they had lubricant and a nurse standing by. And that atrocious jar lifter.

But what might be the lasting effect of this? It was one thing to talk about having a baby. It was another thing to use a giant dildo. It was exactly what he said: a baby going the wrong way.

And what if she liked it? What then? So far in her porn career, she hadn't encountered any organ or act that greatly affected her. But she'd never used a dildo before, ever. And if she liked the kind of instrument waiting for her in the final act, there would never really be any substitute. She might become addicted to it, and stay home every night like the character she was playing. It would ruin any chance of a relationship.

Then again, she'd never heard of a dildo addict. So there probably weren't any. So what was she worried about?

She was just being silly. A dildo is a dildo is a dildo. And this was a job, nothing more.

The time came for shooting. She took up her place on a couch, and pretended to read a romance novel. Jerry called for quiet on the set.

Action.

3

She told herself that she wasn't going to worry but, the next morning when she rolled out of bed, she immediately started with stretching exercises. She wasn't sure it would help but it couldn't hurt.

She winced when she thought about it. She even thought about backing out. But that would certainly torpedo her porn career. Word gets around. "She's a flake," they would say, "prone to tantrums and nervous breakdowns."

It was probably too late to swap with Christie, and even if she could, she didn't want to. Jerry was right about her horror of bodily fluids. Christie was cast in one grisly pic.

She went to work that morning at Finley and Hochstein, and the day went mostly as usual. Only she found herself distracted at times by the stupidest thing. If one of the attorneys used the expression *big case*, she immediately flashed on the bunker busting dildo. If a secretary, along about lunch, mentioned she had an enormous appetite, she again flashed on the dildo. She was flashing on it all day long. And by the time she got out of the office and was driving home, she realized what it was.

She was afraid.

The dildo wasn't just big, it was scary. And she didn't know what might happen if and when she got it inside her.

Jerry and his big ideas! She fumed as she entered her apartment. And then she thought of it again—*big* ideas. And she saw it.

She almost wished she could start with the big one and get it over with. If it didn't fit, well, then she wasn't up for the job. They'd have to call it off.

But she knew that was unrealistic. There was no way Jerry would go for it. She'd have to take them in order, just as he said.

That night, the girl in makeup remarked how tense she seemed.

Alice shook her head. "It's just work at the law office. There's a—" Big case. "—a lot going on right now."

"Okay. 'Cause if I didn't know better, I'd say you were worried about getting acquainted with those dildos out there."

"No, I've met them before. The big one's named Jerry."

The girl laughed and they finished makeup.

Before shooting, Jerry dropped a bombshell.

"I'm gonna scrap a couple of scenes. I think it makes it too long, and they're boring anyway. So we want to flash forward a week or so. So for the next scene, you've already used the smaller ones and moved up to one of the larger sizes."

"How large?"

He stood there, hands on his hips, and shook his head. "I dunno. What do you think you can take?"

"What can I take? I thought we were doing this gradually!"

"We are, we are. Look, I'm not asking you to do anything painful. Just pick one a few sizes up, something that looks comfortable to you. I just don't want to scenes with every single size. We've got thirty of them. Will you just take a look?"

She went to the cabinet and opened it up. They were kept there all the time. No point in putting them up and putting them away again after every shooting day.

She reached up for the dildo two spots over from the .50 cal, but Jerry interrupted her.

"I don't want to pressure you but will you please be a little more ambitious than that? The way the scene works, it's been over a week. You must have used more than the first two during that period of time, right?"

She got flustered. "Well, I don't know! How often am I using them?"

"As often as possible. Every day, at least. You like it. Please. Play along."

She sighed and selected number five. "Okay?"

"That'll do."

In scene two, she had to field another call from her boyfriend, who still hadn't appeared on screen. He was missing her but she—sniff, sniff! cough, cough!—still wasn't feeling well. Maybe next week.

After that she had to do a bedroom scene.

For a change, she had a really pretty bed to work on. Jerry reasoned that as along as it wasn't going to get semen on it, they might as well have the good stuff.

It was a baby-blue king size with big froofy pillows, a lacy bed skirt and silky sheets. At the start of the scene, she had to place the dildo with loving care in the middle of the coverlet and look eagerly at it as she undressed.

She told him before shooting that this was preposterous but he didn't seem to care.

He said, "You have to remember that this is a character study. This woman has an abnormal personality. And for consistency's sake, it would help if you start treating those dildos like your demon lover sooner rather than later."

She did her best to comply but Jerry called cut before they got halfway through the scene.

She was shocked. She'd been interrupted in a scene before but it was always for some very obvious reason, like one of the actors knocking over a dorm lamp with his foot.

He came over and sat down beside her on the bed. This made her a little uncomfortable, as she was naked and had a dildo in her hand, but she put the dildo aside, put her legs primly together and waited for what he had to say.

He said, "What's up?"

She said, "What do you mean, what's up?"

"I mean, what's going on? You're like the ice queen out here. I ask you to treat a dildo like a demon lover and you're handling it like it's an electric razor. And I know you. You can do this scene. But you're holding back. Why?"

She considered it. "Well, I've never done a masturbation scene before."

"So? You've done every other kind of scene before. Why's this a problem?"

She tried to think. Why was it a problem, exactly?

"Well, when I do other scenes, I just have to pretend to react to other people. Here, I'm—" She groped for words.

"Pleasuring yourself."

"Right."

"And?"

"And I don't want other people to see me do that. I mean, I don't know how to pretend with it."

"You mean, you don't know how to pretend to pleasure yourself convincingly without actually doing it. And you don't want to do that in front of us."

There were a half-dozen people standing around.

"Basically, yeah."

She actually thought there might be more to it than that. Thinking about the last dildo on the shelf had her stomach in knots. But using the dildos in front of other people was a problem, too.

"Okay, I guess I understand that. But look, someone has to work the cameras." There were three cameras set up. Jerry liked to get the most out of a scene and sometimes edited his films to replay the same acts from three different angles.

She said, "I just wish I couldn't see any of you. At least then I could pretend you weren't there."

"Okay, if I arrange to make us inconspicuous—and that'll take a few minutes—will you perform for me?"

She said she would.

They ended up running a couple of lines along the stage and draping sheets over them. The only thing that showed from the set were the lenses of the cameras. There was a handheld that they also used but Jerry promised to keep it out of this scene.

Music was often played during scenes, not just on the soundtrack but on the stage. It helped the actors. On this occasion, they turned it up a little louder than usual.

She got down to work.

When it was over and she was dressed, she was curious enough to go over to Jerry and ask, "How did I do?"

He gave her a broad grin and a thumb's up. "You were perfect. Do it like that every time and we'll have a masterpiece."

She felt her face flush. She turned away and got out of the building as quickly as she could.

4

The next night of shooting was longer but easier. The first part took place at a grocery. Jerry couldn't get permission to shoot at a Kroger, Meijer, Aldi or any other other major chain but he'd managed to get them time at a halal market.

The dialogue for the scene was innocuous enough out of context but he warned them all to keep their mouths shut and no joking around. If the owner asked what the movie was about, they were to say it was about social status in a small town.

And the scene was simple. The protagonist (whose name was Katie) meets her friend Rachel at the grocery. Rachel's pleased to see her, because they haven't met in a while. Katie, where have you been? You should get out more. Oh, says Katie, I've been recovering from the flu. I probably wouldn't be out now if I hadn't taken three or four Sudafed. Rachel lets her know that a bunch of the girls are getting together Friday. She, Katie, should join them. Oh, I'd love to but I can't. I probably won't be well by then, and I have a heap of housework to get caught up on. They go back and forth. She couldn't. She just couldn't. She has so much work to do.

The next scene was back at the cabinet. But this time, before choosing her ammo, she strolls down to the bunker buster, takes it in her hands and fondles it, marvels over it, and finally sighs wistfully before putting it back on the shelf. Not ready for that one yet.

She takes down number eight.

Though larger, the incremental difference didn't pose a problem. There was no discomfort, much less pain. And as far as her performance was concerned, she gathered from Jerry's expression afterward that she'd carried it off with aplomb.

The only time she almost fell out of character was when she was standing at the cabinet. Per the script, she'd walked down the whole row of dildos, looking at them as they passed.

Her stomach dropped. There were so many more ahead. Twenty-two after tonight, each one larger than the last. Would she have to use them all? Probably not. They'd already skipped a few. But was that good or bad? She didn't like to think having to run through all of them. But then she didn't want to go bounding ahead, either.

She looked at one about two-thirds down. It seemed comically, implausibly large.

Whenever they did a selection scene, Jerry always had a penny under the dildo she was supposed to choose. It wasn't visible in the shot but she could see as she stood at the cabinet how the designated dildo stood off the shelf a little more than the rest.

How many nights before the penny sat under number twenty-two?

How many nights before it sat under thirty?

5

It was impossible for Alice to make a movie about dildos without wondering how many women used them.

She searched online and found a study that said that a little more than half of American women had used them alone or with a partner. They were more likely to use them for clitoral stimulation than to actually put them inside them, though two-thirds of those who used them did that, too.

The movie was mainly interested in the latter. In fact, putting it inside her was the only thing she was ever explicitly directed to do with it. When she mentioned this to Jerry, he told her do whatever worked for her but always to finish by getting it in.

"We don't have a movie without that."

She also learned that women in relationships were more likely to use one than women who were single. At first blush, the movie seemed in line with this. But it really wasn't. Her character was in a relationship but it was doomed by dildo addiction. So she was a singleton waiting to happen.

The dildos in the movie weren't always on the shelf. Besides using them in scenes, they were also set aside for cleaning. At the end of the shoot, she had to take the dildo to a jar, fill it up with Everclear and screw the lid on. When she showed up the next night, the dildo was dried and back in its spot on the shelf, the jar empty and the bottle of Everclear standing by for the next cleaning.

Jerry told her a story about this.

She was finishing up for the night and just pouring Everclear over dildo number eight when he sidled up to her, leaned over and said, "You know what happens to that Everclear?"

She stared at him.

He jerked his head toward Tom who did the lighting.

He said, "Tom pours it in a thermos. Takes it home and makes cocktails with it."

"That's not true. That's disgusting." She didn't know which of those things mattered more.

"It is true. And what's disgusting? You ever have a guy with his tongue inside you? But who am I asking? Of course, you have. What's the difference?"

She thought there was a difference.

"I don't know. It's creepy."

Jerry shrugged. "This guy's watching a beautiful girl get undressed every night and have fun with herself. He can't touch you. Maybe he likes to think about it."

She didn't know why Jerry told her that story. It probably wasn't true but she couldn't bring herself to ask Tom if it was. He almost certainly wouldn't admit it even if it were true, which made the question pointless. And if he did admit it, she'd never be able to look at him again.

Either way, the story got into her head and she thought of it every time she saw him. It was just weird. Sometimes Jerry went too far.

But what was she thinking? He always went too far.

On the fourth day of shooting, she used number ten.

6

Alice hadn't been kidding when she said that masturbating in front of a camera made her self-conscious. So when he warned her that they'd be using the handheld soon, she got twice as wound up as before. She really didn't want somebody standing near her while she did it.

His justification was that, further the movie went along, the more important it was to capture everything—her body, her hand, the dildo, her face. He wanted it all. And to get it right, according to Jerry, they needed the handheld.

She made a decision. If she was going to carry it off with someone standing beside her, she needed to practice.

She supposed she could have borrowed one from set but she didn't want to. Everyone would put one and one together, and assume that she'd developed a taste for it. Not that there was anything wrong with that. But she'd have to field jokes about how they didn't see her out and about much anymore, and her friends missed her, and she must be coming down with the sniffles.

So she went to the store.

This proved as uncomfortable as masturbating in front of other people. The clerk was a woman, which made it worse somehow.

Despite having made seven pornos, she'd never actually been in an adult bookstore before. And making pornos hadn't encouraged her. Once she knew there was a movie out there with her face in it, the last thing she'd wanted to do was waltz into a store where it might be sitting on a shelf.

The shop had, among other things, a row of glass cases with various objects inside. For a while, Alice was lost in looking at them. Nipple clamps, butt plugs, ball gags, furry handcuffs, leather masks, whips, inflatable dolls, and dozens of other things, some of which she couldn't identify at all.

The clerk said, "Can I help you find something?"

"No, thanks," Alice answered with what she felt like a frozen, deer-in-the-headlights smile. "I'm just looking."

After that, she decided to get down to business, and that meant browsing the dildos. She moved down to where a vast assortment of them stood behind the glass. She peeked at the clerk but that nice lady seemed to be ignoring her. She was watching a game show.

In a Spanish translation of this novel, chapter one begins, "Era el mejor de los tiempos, era el peor de los teimpos."

A Tale of Two Cities, she thought, remembering it from school. Then she concentrated on the dildos.

It should have been easy but instead she was confused. All of the dildos for the movie were anatomically modeled, with flat bases. But the ones in the case here were more varied and technical somehow. There were some with wide bases and narrow projections to the tip. Some had ribs or ridges. Some had two heads. Some were glassy. They seemed to be made of all kinds of materials. She didn't know how to choose.

If she were shopping for almost anything else, she might've asked the clerk to make a recommendation. As it was, she just picked one that looked similar to what she was working with and called over the clerk to get it for her.

The clerk, who till now had been discreet and unobtrusive, ventured, "My, that's a big one! Someone's going to have a good time!"

She flushed but said nothing. She just paid and got out of the store.

It wasn't even as big as number ten.

7

Back in the movie, Katie's habit was getting a little out of hand.

This was a case where the scenes were indeed shot a little out of order. It wasn't till ten at night that they shot the one that took place first.

Katie's preparing to go to work as a receptionist at an unspecified business. She applies her makeup, puts on her jacket, and grabs her purse.

She's just about to walk out the door when she pauses and looks back at the cabinet. Then she slowly walks toward it, opens it, and surveys her collection.

She checks her watch and frowns. She looks at the door to her apartment, then back at the cabinet. Then she grabs number twelve and hurries over to the couch. She dumps her purse out onto a cushion and stuffs the dildo at the bottom of it. Then she carefully but hurriedly packs the purse again.

Then she hurries out the door.

The next bit was shot earlier in the night.

This was shot at the front desk at an office called Yard and Associates. It was a law firm. It was after hours but one of the lawyers was on hand to watch. According to Jerry, he thought they were shooting a low-budget horror movie. But she wondered. It was a little too close to reality. She worked at a law office. This was a law office. She wondered if Mr. Yard or whoever he was happened to know her employers.

In the scene, she takes a call, then is told by one of the lawyers (played by Jerry) that she could go to lunch. She walks down an empty hallway, apparently going out to eat. But then she comes to an office door. It's unlocked and dark inside. She looks both ways in the hallway, then goes inside, locking the door behind her.

After that, they shot a scene with someone trying the handle of the door and knocking. After half a minute, Katie emerges, apologizing that she'd stopped to sort through her purse, and the door must've automatically locked behind her.

The rest was shot back at the sound stage, performed mostly in a wheeled chair with her feet propped up on a conference table until the end when, losing herself in the moment, she clambered on top of the table and finished in a position that was convenient to the cameras.

Again, there's a knocking. She hurrries down from the table, arranges herself, and frantically stows the dildo away in the purse that she manages to get zipped just before she reaches the door.

The next day was a Saturday, so she was off from Finley and Hochstein. And since shooting didn't start till seven, she had most of the day to herself.

She occupied much of her time in chores. But along about one in the afternoon, her mind wandered back to the movie.

She'd used the dildo she bought, and using one when she was alone had helped when she had to use one for the camera. Since then, the masturbation scenes hadn't been nearly as nerve-racking for her as they were before.

She was still a little concerned about the progression ahead of her. Maybe she should buy a larger one, try to get ahead of the problem, or at least find out if it was a problem.

But she didn't want to go back to the store. If the clerk thought the last one was big, her eyes would pop out at what Alice was looking for now. And as a matter of fact, she wasn't sure the store had anything of the proper size.

So she went online and did a little shopping. By now, she had a good idea of the dimensions of the dildos she would be using. After looking for a while, she found something that looked like number 18. It was the largest she could find.

She impulsively clicked *Buy*, and then somewhat less impulsively entered her address and credit card info.

By the time all this was done, she'd been thinking about dildos for the better part of an hour.

She'd enjoyed it when she used the dildo alone, in a way that was completely different from her sensations on camera. She didn't want to enjoy herself when people were staring at her. But in privacy, with no one around, it wasn't that bad.

She went to her room and opened a drawer. It couldn't hurt. And with two weeks of shooting left, she might as well get used to it.

8

Scripts for pornos—at least the ones Alice had been in—were flexible to the whims and intuitions of the director. In the present case, Jerry's intuition had led him to the conclusion that the movie's premise had been well established and that therefore the further mechanical progression of plot could be replaced with a more impressionistic approach.

What this meant in practice was that Alice was called on to shoot a series of very short scenes in which she told her boyfriend over and over again that she had a headache, only to hurry over—once the door was closed behind her—to the cabinet where she kept her shining pretties. And then, having selected her partner for the night, she retired to her bed where she diddled herself passionately, loudly and in streaming tears of joy in scenes that were comparatively long and shot from numerous angles.

During lunch breaks, she read the newspaper, paying particular attention to foreign affairs. It seemed the right counterbalance to a morning spent in masturbation. And it communicated to her co-workers that she wasn't a one-dimensional lady. She had depth, interests, wide-ranging concerns. Dildo diddling was only one side of her.

Anyway, that was for her co-workers. But on her own time and in private, she was increasingly troubled. It wasn't something she could've explained. But she was constantly and irrationally distracted by the thought of the movie, or rather by the subject of the movie. More specifically she was distracted by the thought of the size 18 "smooth criminal" stowed away in her underwear drawer.

Size 18 might not sound like much but it was no joke. The day the package arrived from Amazon, she took it out and put it in the drawer, intending to use it at the next opportunity. But it lay there for almost an entire day before she worked up the nerve to try it.

If only Jerry knew. She was ahead of filming.

But she felt she had to use it. Never mind whether Jerry appreciated the effort she made on her own time to get into the role. It was a matter of self-respect. It was research, rehearsal, character study. Hell, she was transcending her genre. She was a method actor! Had any porn star ever gone so far to acquaint herself with the delights of dildos? She thought not.

She was intent on one thing and one thing only: knowledge—knowledge of what such a character as she portrayed might think or feel if she, the character, actually enjoyed—indeed, was obsessed by—the frequent and vigorous use of a dildo.

Of course, if her character were really obsessed with masturbation, she would probably buy a vibrator. True, it wasn't in the script but the script was written by a small-minded, beady-eyed fellow who didn't appreciate the themes of his own movie. It was the story of a woman in search of physical fulfillment—he got that much. But he didn't seem to realize that it wasn't just a stunt but an odyssey, a pilgrimage to onanistic paradise. It was the transformation of a soul from chrysalis to butterfly.

It was time to make a stand. She got out the smooth operator and set to work.

9

"Ahh! Ah, god. God. Ahh!"

Beads of sweat stood out on her forehead. She was rehearsing. She had to remember that. Be professional.

"Oh my god."

She thought distractedly that it was ridiculous. It was asking too much from an actor to get this deep into a role.

Two hours later, she was dressed and on her way to work at her night job, about as well prepared as she could be.

Back on set, she buttonholed Jerry before going into makeup.

"What do you want? I'm busy."

"I think my character should use a vibrator."

"What? Why?"

"It's an exploration of personal pleasure. It's the logical next step."

"No. No, it's not the next logical step. The next logical step is the size 17 mastadon. Size, Alice! It's the whole point of the movie."

"I know. But it shouldn't be. Size isn't everything!"

He smiled. "You give hope to men everywhere. But it doesn't matter. Size is the story's whole concept. We start getting into vibrators and the movie turns into a trade show. Not that that's a bad idea. But it's another movie. If you want, I'll cast you in it. Now leave me alone. I'm busy."

She went to makeup, fuming.

The makeup girl had seen the dustup with Jerry but didn't know what it was about. Alice didn't enlighten her. The whole subject made her uncomfortable and irritable.

This bad mood made the night longer than it had to be. The mastadon, though not precisely too big, created a certain amount of friction. It was distinctly uncomfortable and, as she pointed out to Jerry, if she were forced to continue, she'd probably end up too raw to continue filming.

Someone rustled up a bottle of olive oil from a bodega down the street and after a little cautious experiment she found she was able to continue work.

But Jerry wasn't happy with her performance. He called cut several times and explained to her that the progression in size needed to produce a progressive reaction. She needed to emote, show anticipation, fear, struggle, pain, joy. She was climbing Mount Everest. The audience needed to see that. Otherwise, there's no real buildup and the movie didn't work.

So she had to do the scene over and over again.

What made it worse was that she'd somehow become emotionally invested in the role in a way she hadn't with previous films. She wanted it to be a realistic and humane portrayal. And she felt as if the character were being made to use dildos on demand and on someone else's schedule. Which was exactly what was happening!

It was outrageous but somehow, after six or seven takes, she found herself disappearing into the character. No thanks to script or direction, she managed to get a performance out of it.

When it was done, Jerry came over.

"Well, it wasn't as loud as I'd envisioned it but I have to admit, you were convincing. What gave you the idea to make your lip tremble like that?"

She was still sore at him. "I thought a little bit about the character. You should try it sometime."

"Maybe so. But since when are you such a critic of characters in my movies? Where's the simple girl of six months ago who was happy with maids' outfits and money shots?"

"She grew up. You should try it."

"Can't afford it. Got pornos to make. Well, see you tomorrow. And for what it's worth, we're almost done. And then you can move on to work more deserving of your talents. I hear Latex Films is casting something called *I was a Sex-Starved Terrorist*."

She couldn't think of a time when she was so anxious to get away from set. She wiped off the olive oil before leaving but wouldn't feel clean till she'd taken a shower.

But it was more than that. She'd never been a big fan of J. Gerald Peterson but in the past few days, she'd come to loathe him. Not only that, but she'd come to loathe the whole business.

In the beginning, working pornos had seemed the obvious thing to do. People like to look at other people having sex. She provided the service and got paid for it.

But now it seemed supremely unnatural. If sex wasn't private, what was? Why should she show herself to people while she had sex? It wasn't a performance. Well, it was, but it shouldn't be. That's not what it was meant for.

Even after a hot shower, she was jittery and unhappy. She wished she could disappear somewhere. She didn't even feel like going in to the law firm tomorrow. But she had to. She had to pay the bills.

There was a half-finished bottle of wine in the fridge. While she tried to think about her future, she finished it.

The whole reason she'd considered doing pornos to begin with was because she thought it wouldn't make any difference. She'd had a few relationships in her young life and none of them had gone anywhere. Or rather, they gone to sex, stayed there a while, then ended abruptly. A short round-trip to right back to where she started, nothing changed but the mileage.

The plot of the movie was ironic, really. The conceit of it was that her character had a boyfriend who was constantly trying to see her. But she couldn't be bothered because she was holed up with her dildo. But if her boyfriend was really as attentive and sincere as he was portrayed, Alice imagined the dildos wouldn't be very important.

But then there'd be no movie. Or at least no movie that Jerry would want to make.

The point was, as long as she was giving sex to people who didn't care about her, she might as well be making money from it. It would be a way to hit back. She could make money, become a vet, get a nice house and a dog. And then men wouldn't even enter into it anymore.

And now, here she was, making money. But she wasn't happy.

After the bottle, she felt maudlin and tired. She didn't want to think anymore. Fortunately, she didn't have to. She collapsed on the bed and instantly fell asleep.

10

She woke up late and had to hurry to get to work. But once there, she was happy to be in the ordinary routine of answering calls, updating schedules, entering time billed, and drafting documents and letters. It wasn't her dream job but it wasn't bad. She liked her employer. She was happy there.

She wondered whether she couldn't just save the money for vet school while working one job. She had a head start from the past six months of pornos. Who said she had to do any more?

But when she got home that afternoon, she realized that she still a week away from finishing the current film. She was supposed to be on set that night.

She dreaded it.

The more she thought of it, the more the movie seemed like the most humiliating scenario Jerry could've devised. If she'd only been called on to perform oral sex, it would at least have been ordinary. As it was, she was a one-woman freak show. See what a big dildo she can get inside her! Wow! How big can she go?

It was stupid. As a performance, it was stupid. As a way of working off nerves before a second job, it was great.

As on the previous evening, she managed to disappear into the part. But this time, thankfully, there weren't any cameras around. No one called cut. And the olive oil stayed in the kitchen.

When she was done, she felt much better but also tired. A little nap would help.

She woke at 11:15.

At first, she just marveled that she'd slept for four hours. Then she thought how refreshed she felt. She must've been sleeping poorly and the nap finally made up the deficit.

Then she turned on the lamp, saw the dildo on the night stand, and realized that she late for shooting.

Late! This was beyond late. Shooting was supposed to start at 7:30.

A flurry of thoughts went through her head. Why didn't anyone call her? And if they did, why didn't she wake when the phone rang? But she'd put the phone on mute. She remembered now. She hadn't wanted to be disturbed.

It was too late to call Jerry. He'd be angry and she didn't want to argue at this time of night. But she looked at her phone. There were six calls and three voicemails.

"Alice, this is Jerry. We're waiting. I hope you're on your way."

"Alice. We're all here on set waiting for you. Get your butt down here. Now."

"Alice, this is Jerry. Everybody's going home. I'm telling you this so you won't bother to come down here. See what I did there? I called and let you know I wouldn't be around. Call me tomorrow first thing in the morning and let me know what's up."

This was terrible. She could patch it up, all right. It wasn't as if he'd replace her. But it would be embarrassing to see everyone on set after being a no-show. What would she say when he asked what had happened to her?

She'd overslept, that was all. It was a long day at work, she was tired, and she overslept. It was a lame excuse but plausible.

In the meantime, she had another problem. It was bedtime and she couldn't sleep.

She got up and went to the kitchen. There wasn't anything in the fridge but there was a bottle of red wine in a cabinet. She drank a few glasses while watching TV.

When she felt too tired to watch TV, she went back to bed. But when she lay down, she couldn't sleep. It was like her brain was an empty shop, shuttered and locked for the night. But there was still a light on over the sign, and it wouldn't go out.

She opened her eyes and her glance fell on the dildo still sitting on the night stand. As long as she had to be awake, she might as well enjoy it.

She got to work.

She never could guess how long she was awake that night. But sometime during the proceedings, she fell asleep. When she awoke, the dildo was still in her hand.

And once again, she was running late.

She entered the law office ten minutes after eight and made her profuse apologies to everyone. No one was angry but it raised eyebrows. She was always so punctual.

11

That day at work—the law office—was a trying one. As sometimes happens, a bad start to the day threw everything off kilter

There was more work than usual. She got backed up, confused, made a few mistakes. It was all small potatoes but bothersome. She didn't go to lunch till one-thirty. And when she did, she was so famished, all she could think about was food. Never mind the diet, she wanted comfort—a bacon cheeseburger with plenty of fries.

So it wasn't till three that she remembered Jerry. And it wasn't till an hour later that she could get away from her desk to call him from a stall in the ladies' room.

As soon as he heard her voice, he said, "You were supposed to call me first thing in the morning. You call this first thing in the morning? What time zone are you in?"

She was in a multi-occupant restroom and there was a woman in the next stall, so she whispered.

"I know. I'm sorry. I overslept yesterday and today's been hell at work."

"Oh, sorry to hear that. I had a bad day, too. Worked all night and didn't get a thing done."

"I know, I'm sorry. How many times do you want me to say it?"

"I don't. I just want to know where you're going to be at 7:30 tonight."

"I'll be there."

"I hope so. I'm the forgiving sort, Alice, but you won't work in this industry if you're not reliable."

"I'll be there. I promise."

But when she got home, she wasn't so sure she would be. After everything else that had happened, she was still nervous about the endgame of the film. It wasn't just the practical difficulty, it was the ultimate result of it. What if the film were successful? What if it were famous, notorious, legendary? Did she want that kind of fame? Did her employer watch pornos? Did her neighbors? Why did she ever get mixed up in this at all?

Thinking about it gave her a headache. She took three aspirin but it didn't help. Neither did a glass of wine. She only had an hour before she had to be there.

She had to do something to calm down. Since she had no other ideas, she retreated to the bedroom and got to work.

A half-hour later, sweaty and a little weak of limb, she dragged herself from bed, pulled herself together and drove to the set.

As soon as she arrived, Jerry gave her the schedule of the day's shoot.

"To make up for lost time, we're going a little long tonight. I've decided I want a clutch of scenes showing the deterioration of her social relations. Then we're doing three bed scenes. Then, with any luck, we'll wrap up tomorrow."

"Tomorrow?"

"Yeah, tomorrow. That's good, right? You don't like the movie, anyway. The sooner we get done, the sooner you can move on to a project you respect."

He was still annoyed with her over her criticisms and her failure to show up.

"Of course, I want to get done. But aren't we moving a little fast? I thought we were working up gradually."

He cocked an eyebrow. "We have. Maybe you haven't noticed it but you've covered a lot of ground. Once you got started, you took the 17 like it was nothing. Trust me, Alice. This isn't going to be a problem for you."

This was unsettling news. Had she really gone so far? After makeup, she made time to peek into the cabinet.

There they all were. And he was right. The bunker-buster was huge. But maybe she could take it.

This didn't make her feel less nervous. If anything, she felt as if she'd lost control of herself. A couple of weeks ago, the whole prospect was ridiculous. Now it was real.

Her nervousness played well in the scenes they had to shoot.

Katie meets her friends again in the supermarket.

"Goodness, where have you been? We never see you anymore."

"Oh, busy."

"With what?"

"Stuff."

"Stuff like what?"

"Work. Working long hours."

"Oh? Why long hours all of a sudden?"

"Lots of cases. Big cases. Very big cases."

Her mother calls.

"Sorry, I missed Thanksgiving, mom. I've just been so busy. Cases. Lots of cases. Very big cases."

Her boyfriend pays a visit.

"What's going on? I haven't seen you for weeks. You don't answer my calls."

"I've wanted to call. But I've been exhausted. Work's been hell. And the little time I've had off I've spent getting caught up on chores."

"Housework?"

"Yes."

"But everything's covered with dust, your clothes are scattered on the floor, there are three empty pizza boxes on the couch and there are cobwebs on your coffee table."

"I'm not caught up yet."

"Tell me the truth! What's really going on?"

"Nothing. I've just been really busy."

"Are you telling me the truth? You're not seeing someone else?"

"No, of course not."

"Well, then can you see me tonight?"

"Uh, yes, of course."

"Great, then let's have dinner together."

"All right, let's go."

There's no restaurant scene. Instead, they return to her apartment, talking as they come through the door.

The boyfriend said, "It's no wonder they do such a good business. I couldn't believe the size of that steak."

"Yes, it was—enormous."

"I liked the dessert, too. Didn't you?"

"Yes, it was delicious."

"The apple pie was great but that pudding cake looked even better."

"Yes, it was good."

"It looked so buttery and moist."

"Yes, it is—I mean, was. Uh, help yourself to a drink. I'll be back in a few minutes. I just need to freshen up."

For once, there was a scene shot without Alice. The boyfriend sits in the living room, waiting. He drinks his drink. Clinks the cubes idly, still waiting. Refills his drink, looks at his watch, taps his foot.

Finally, he calls out. "Alice? Alice?"

He marches down the hall.

For the next scene, she's back in bed, working away with the size 20 "Big Log." She's got her feet up on the footboard and is quietly moaning when the boyfriend bursts into the room.

There's an emotional scene. So this is what you've been doing with all your time. Cheating on me with an inanimate object! Can't even wait till I'm gone! And—dear god, woman, how do you even get that thing inside you?

She pleads her case. She didn't mean it to go this far. It was an accident. She was just curious. And it got out of control. Now that she's seen him again, this'll be the last time. Only please, please, go back to the living room and give her ten, fifteen more minutes.

He doesn't believe her. She has a problem. An addiction! She needs help.

But she loves him. She really does. She just doesn't know how to stop.

Contemptuous, disgusted, he leaves. He never wants to see her again.

Now alone, she's distraught, weeping. What can she do?

She staggers to the living room, unlocks the cabinet. Still weeping, she gazes at her collection, takes down the size 20.

"You're all I have left now. We're alone in the world." She clutches it to her face and the tears stream down.

The next three scenes were meant to cover sizes 21, 23 and 25. But first, they'd break for lunch.

The set emptied out. The girl from makeup asked, "Are you going to grab a bite with us?"

Alice wasn't hungry.

They went out and she was alone.

12

Left to her own devices, Alice became bored and restless. And something of the desperate unhappiness of her character had communicated itself to her.

The crew would probably be gone for a whole hour.

She checked her purse. There was nothing there.

Well, that entirely wasn't true. There was a card case, a change purse, a key ring, a cell phone, a can of pepper spray, a comb and brush, a small bottle of hair spray, chewing gum, a bottle of perfume, and a thousand other things.

But it didn't contain what she was looking for.

She looked at the cabinet. It was still unlocked.

She took down the 21 and sighed. Two weeks ago, she would've said it was impractical. But it wasn't. She was sure of that now.

She looked around, trying to think where she should go. But then she realized she was being stupid. Everyone was gone. She should use the bed.

In a half hour, the size 21 was back in its place. Alice was dressed and seated beside the little table with the coffee pot for the crew. She sipped from her cup as the crew returned.

The rest of the night went surprisingly smoothly. 21, 23, 25. And she performed with gusto, gave it all she had. She expressed herself freely—grunting, groaning, whimpering, moaning, sighing, gasping. And when her character clearly couldn't take it any more, she opened her eyes wide and made a strangled choking sound, arched her back and froze like that for a count of five before collapsing like a dead woman onto the sweat-bedewed sheets of her satiated lust.

Jerry called cut.

This was immediately followed by a shocking sound of applause. The entire crew, Jerry, the actor who played her boyfriend, even the girl who did makeup and wardrobe, were giving her a standing ovation. They obviously thought she'd done something special.

She was still taking this in when Jerry came over to congratulate her.

"Alice, dear. You've just made history."

"How? We haven't even finished."

"Doesn't matter. No matter how we end this thing, we've made a work of art. Trust me, when we get all this through post-production, properly cut and some music behind it, it's going to be worth its weight in gold."

"You think so?"

"I know so. Trust me, kid. You're going to be famous."

She didn't like that. She didn't want to be famous, not this way. She didn't want to be known as the Moby Dick of dildo wielders. She wanted out of the business. She wanted a regular life as a secretary or a vet.

She looked around helplessly as though someone might tell her what to do. But her eyes only met Tom the cameraman. He was picking up the 25 and dropping it into a jar of everclear. He winked at her.

She got out of there as fast as she could. This was the end. No more pornos. And if there were going to be any more dildos, they'd stay in the privacy of her own room.

As soon as she made that decision, the weight of the world seemed to lift from her shoulders. She felt happy and buoyant. She would go to her regular job tomorrow and have a regular day. After work, maybe she'd get a pint of ice cream and watch a movie.

Whatever she did, it would be just fine. She'd seen the last of J. Gerald Peterson and My Goodness Productions.

13

She woke early for a change, got ready for work, even made a light breakfast instead of just brewing a thermos of coffee and rushing out the door.

As she ate, she realized there was something she should do. It wasn't much, and wouldn't be pleasant, but it seemed the honorable thing.

She called Jerry.

He said, "You really baffle me, you know that? I ask you to call first thing in the morning and you call at closing time. Now you're ringing me at seven in the morning. What's up?"

"Jerry, I'm sorry but I'm quitting the film."

"What?"

"You heard me. I can't do this any more."

"But why? We're almost finished."

She could've tried to explain. But there was no way he would understand. And arguing would just be painful.

"It doesn't matter. The point is, I'm out. I know you wanted notice if I wasn't going to be there. Well, I'm not going to be there. Bye, Jerry."

"Alice, wait—"

She hung up, then blocked his number. She knew he'd call back.

It was a relief to work an ordinary day at the office. Everything went without a hitch. She ate lunch with the girls. And when she got off, she decided to get that pint of ice cream.

And she was just coming down the hallway to her apartment with a bag of rocky road cradled in her arm when she saw him waiting for her. It was Jerry.

"What are you doing here?"

"We need to talk."

"No, we don't. Go away."

"Alice, I'm sorry. I am. But please, hear me out. If you don't want to do the movie, I understand. I just want you to hear me for a few minutes."

She didn't like this.

"Please? And then I'll leave."

"Make it quick." She keyed open the door and they went in.

She put the ice cream in the freezer. He stood by the couch, waiting for her. If he thought she would come over and they'd sit down together, he was mistaken. She stood in the kitchenette with her arms folded.

"So what do you want?"

"First of all, I want to apologize. Last night, I made a mistake. I drove you too hard. I put you under too much pressure. And I didn't realize what the film meant to you."

"What do you mean, meant to me?"

"I mean, I realize now that you were more invested than I thought. You really cared about that character."

"I told you that before. You ignored me."

"I did. But I shouldn't have. I'm sorry."

"Because I dropped out of the movie and you want me to come back."

"I admit, I do want you to come back. But that's not what changed my mind."

"Then what did?"

He looked uncomfortable. "Well, it just sort of settled on me that you were really sincere. I mean, at first, I just thought you were being a prima donna. You know, an actress—difficult. But I don't think that any more. I think you had your heart in it."

"Why?"

"I just do. I see it now."

"I believe you see it. But *how* do you see it?"

"Alice, this isn't my fault. Do you promise not to get mad?"

"I won't promise but I'll try."

"You remember when we all went out to lunch last night?"

She didn't answer.

He went on. "The thing is, that place has security cameras. Not a lot of them but a few, enough to cover most of the interior of the building. I admit I couldn't make out much detail. I mean, you can magnify it but at a certain point, it gets pixelated and fuzzy and you don't get much detail. But you can make out the movement—"

"You saw me!"

"Yes. But not because I wanted to."

"Oh, no, I'll bet it was really hard work for you to look at."

"One of my guys was looking at the footage and he told me. That was how I saw it."

"One of your guys. Tom?"

"Let's not bring names into it, okay?"

"No, lets! He was spying on me."

"To be fair, you were doing it on set. Most people wait till they get home."

She ran a hand over her face. He was right. She should've waited.

"So what's the point of telling me this?"

"I just wanted to know that I understood. About caring about the character."

"You think you understand?"

"Well, sure. I mean, the part's got what you might call autobiographical connotations for you, right?"

"That's not what it is!"

"Well, then what is it?"

"Jerry, the part's humiliating."

"How?"

"How? How? Well, let's see. In the last scenes of the moie, you have me bring out the bunker buster by candlelight, like some kind of witches' sabbath, making love to it and mooning over it while the music from *2001* plays in the background—"

"Also Sprach Zarathustra."

"What?"

"Also Sprach—"

"Jerry."

"Okay."

"And then, when I've fitted it in and gotten well underway diddling myself with it, a drumbeat starts, which merges into the pounding of a door. And at the climactic moment—at *my* climactic moment—the door bursts open and my boyfriend, family, friends and co-workers all rush into the room to perform an intervention. They tear me away from the grand-daddy of all dildos and bundle me out of the room. Finally, in the last scene, people talk in hushed tones about how sad it is what happened to me, my unfortunate obsession, my delirium, my madness. And it cuts away to me in a straightjacket, grinning like a loon and shouting, 'Bigger! Bigger! BIGGERRRR!' And that's the end of the movie."

"Not quite. We've got that musical montage of you using all the dildos during closing credits."

"Jerry, it's stupid, childish, demeaning and ludicrous. I don't want to do it. I won't! And I'm never doing a porno again."

Jerry hung his head. She was surprised at this reaction. He seemed totally defeated, like a whipped child.

She should've known better. He was just thinking.

He said, "What if it didn't end that way?"

"What?"

He looked up, grinning like a loon.

"What if I let you rewrite it?"

14

In the end, they compromised. Jerry got a little of his scene with the bunker buster. No candlelight, no Richard Strauss. But she brought it out, worked with it a while, then collapsed on the bed in tears. It was all so pointless. She soliloquized a few lines. What good was it to obtain exquisite pleasure with giant dildos if you had to be alone all your life?

Maybe there was still a chance. She called her boyfriend. No answer. He was probably blocking her calls and never wanted to hear from her again. She'd lost him forever.

She tried to contain her desperation. She was alone. She'd always be alone. Her only comfort—she looked toward the cabinet—but no. She had to renounce it all, try to rebuild her life.

But she was alone. What could she do?

She went back to the cabinet. Look at them all. At least she could have pleasure. At least she could drown her sorrow. At least—

The doorbell rang. It was him. She falls into his arms. She confesses her weakness and says she never wants to see a dildo again—at least, she adds cheekily, not unless he's in the room with her.

The happily reunited lovers kiss and embrace. He goes into the next room and returns with a trash can, carries it to the cabinet and looks at her hopefully. Using two hands, she takes every one of them down and throws them inside.

They embrace again and the movie ends on their embrace.

When it was done, Jerry invited her to the wrap party.

"Thanks, but I really think it's better if I didn't. I need to move on with my life. And the sooner I put all this behind me, the better."

"Well, if you say so. Anyway, thanks for coming back to finish. And good luck."

Jerry lit a cigar.

It wasn't quite the ending he'd hoped for but at least it got done. Endings are overrated anyway. If you can get 'em for the first hour, you got 'em for the whole ride. There was no doubt in his mind that high-concept porn was the next big thing and *Dildo of Doom* would be a big success.

He was still smoking when he overheard a couple of crew members talking.

One of them said, "I don't know why they always carry so much. You'd think they'd throw their backs out."

Jerry was curious. "Who would throw their backs out?"

"Women. They carry so much in their purses."

"Do they? Yeah, I guess they do. But what brought this up?"

"I just saw Alice walking out. I guess she's not coming to the wrap party. Anyway, she looked like she was carrying cannon balls in that bag of hers. I guess it wasn't too heavy, though. She seemed to be shouldering it all right."

Jerry didn't listen any more. He had a hunch.

He strolled back onto set, even as everything was being taken down. He looked inside the trash can.

Inside were 20 dildos. The other 10 had taken a walk. Including Big Bertha.

He should've known.